SQUARE
FISH

An Imprint of Macmillan

HERE COMES JACK FROST. Copyright © 2009 by Kazuno Kohara. All rights reserved.
Printed in June 2011 in China by Shenzhen Wing King Tong Paper Products Company Ltd.,
Shenzhen, Guangdong Province. For information, address
Square Fish, 175 Fifth Avenue, New York, NY 10010.

Square Fish and the Square Fish logo are trademarks of Macmillan and
are used by Roaring Brook Press under license from Macmillan.

Cataloging-in-Publication Data is on file at the Library of Congress
ISBN 978-0-312-60446-2

First published in Great Britain by Macmillan Children's Books, London
Originally published in the United States by Roaring Brook Press
First Square Fish Edition: October 2011
Square Fish logo designed by Filomena Tuosto
mackids.com

10 9 8 7 6 5 4 3 2 1

AR: 1.9

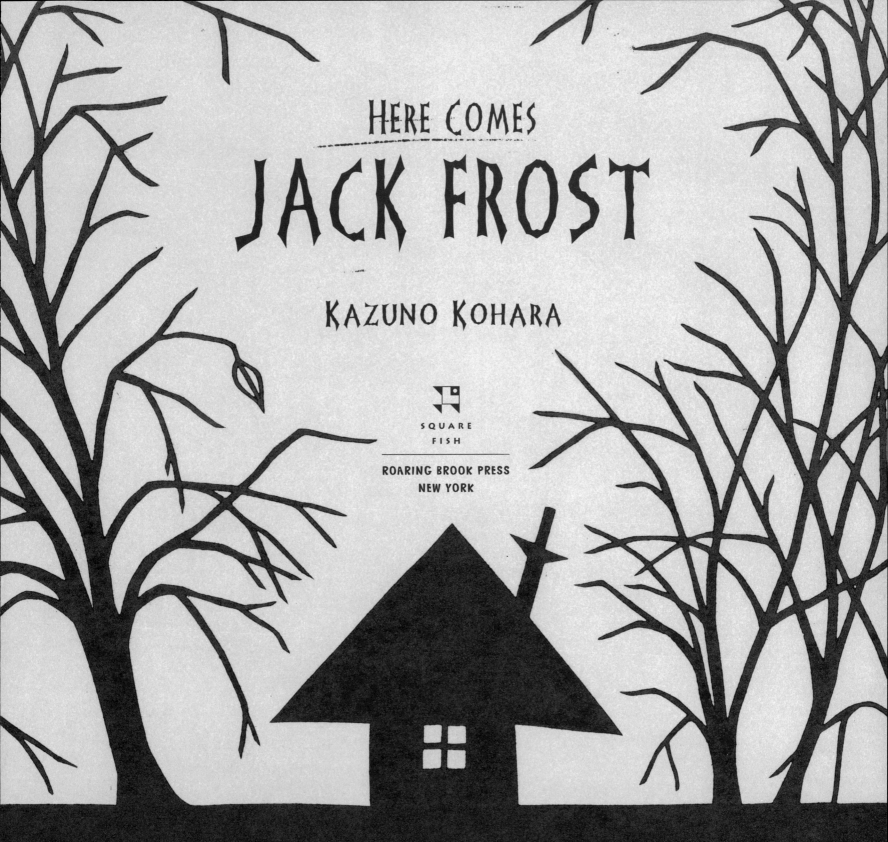

HERE COMES
JACK FROST

KAZUNO KOHARA

SQUARE
FISH

ROARING BROOK PRESS
NEW YORK

Once there was a boy who lived in a house in the woods. It was winter, and all his friends were hibernating.

"I hate winter," he sighed.

But then, one cold morning . . .

. . . **strange patterns
appeared on the window!**

The boy ran outside, and saw a white figure
covering his house with frost and ice.

"Who are you?" asked the boy.

"I'm Jack Frost!" replied the figure,

and he ran into the woods.
"Wait!" cried the boy, and chased after him.

"You can't catch me!"
laughed Jack Frost.
"You can't jump over
the pond!"

But the boy had ice skates.

"You can't catch me!"
cried Jack Frost.
"You can't jump over
the hill!"

But the boy had a sled.

Jack Frost threw a snowball at the boy.
He threw one back!

And another . . .

and another.

It was fun!

"Will you stay and play with me?" asked the boy.
"Yes," smiled Jack Frost, "but never mention
anything warm in front of me . . .

**that would break the spell
and force me to leave. But now
there are so many things we can do."**

"I know," said the boy. "Let's build snowmen!"

They built three, so that they wouldn't feel lonely.

All winter, the boy was careful not to mention anything warm.

Until one day . . .

They were playing
hide-and-seek in the woods when
the boy found something.

It was a snowdrop.

"Look, Jack Frost!" said the boy.

"It's almost spring . . ."

But Jack Frost was
no longer there.
The spell was broken.

But in the wind that went
through the woods,
the boy was sure he heard
a whisper . . .

"See you next winter!"